I JUST WANT TO FLIP

JELP SHINHOLSTER IV

ISBN: 978-1-63944-548-6 (paperback)
ISBN: 978-1-63944-550-9 (hardcover)

First Edition Book, September 2021

Book cover design, illustration, editing, and interior layout by:

www.1000storybooks.com

Hi! My name is Jelp.

It's pronounced like "help" but with a J. My family and friends call me JD.

My Dad is my best friend and we have so much fun together.

He always plays with me and teaches me so many things.

Oh, just a minute, he's calling me.

"Be yourself
everyone
else is
already
taken"
BE KiNDER
THAN
NECESSARY

"Hey JD, let's go shoot some hoops in the driveway before school."

"Okay Dad, be right there!"

My Dad and I play a lot of sports together.

"Okay Dad, I have to head to school now."

"Okay, see you later. Maybe we can throw the football around when you get home."

“Sure Dad!”

On Sundays, after we come home from church service, my Dad and I usually play catch.

My Dad bought me a new baseball glove last week for my birthday.

It is black with white seams.

One day after we were done playing catch, my Dad asked me, "Out of all the different sports that we play, which one is your favorite?"

I answered, "Well, Dad ... none, really. I just want to flip. Dad, can I show you my cartwheel? Can I try Gymnastics?"

"Gymnastics! Well, I don't know son...let Mommy and I talk about it."

After I went to bed that night, my Mom and Dad sat down at the dining room table.

My Mom was curious and asked , "How does JD even know about gymnastics?"

My Dad replies, "I am not sure, maybe he saw some videos on the internet."

We have a lot to learn.

So, my Mom and Dad decided to go on the internet to look up a few things.

They tried to find a gymnastics studio in the area that had classes for boys like me.

The next morning after breakfast, my Dad called me into the living room to show me something.

"Hey JD! Mommy and I found a gymnastics studio close by that offers a beginner boys' class on Saturdays."

Wow! I was so happy.

PRAYERS

Then Saturday came, I was so excited and a little nervous too.

My tummy felt like it had butterflies inside.

I could not believe I was about to start my first gymnastics class.

All I could think about was doing cartwheels, handstands and learning how to do a backflip.

5 REASONS YOUR SON SHOULD DO GYMNASTICS

(EVEN IF HE DOESN'T WANT TO BE A GYMNAST)

- Gymnastics is the perfect foundation for all sports.
- Gymnastics is the perfect cross training sport.
- Gymnastics is the perfect injury prevention program.
- Gymnastics is the perfect character building sport.
- Gymnastics is the perfect sport to learn to be coachable.

My eyes lit up as we entered the gymnastics studio.

All of the lights were so bright.

I was overwhelmed by the sight of the equipment, team trophies and photos of past and present gymnasts.

Most of the walls showed pictures of girls, however there were a few pictures of boys with medals around their necks.

When I looked up at my Dad, I saw him reading a poster titled, 5 Reasons Your Son Should Do Gymnastics (Even If He Doesn't Want To Be A Gymnast).

While in beginner boys' gymnastics class, I learned basic skills on the Pommel Horse, Rings, Balance Beam and High Bar.

I quickly learned that there is much more to gymnastics than just doing cartwheels and flipping.

We start each class with stretching to loosen and warm up our muscles to reduce the risk of us getting hurt.

I really enjoy learning all of these new things about gymnastics because I really want to become the best that I can be.

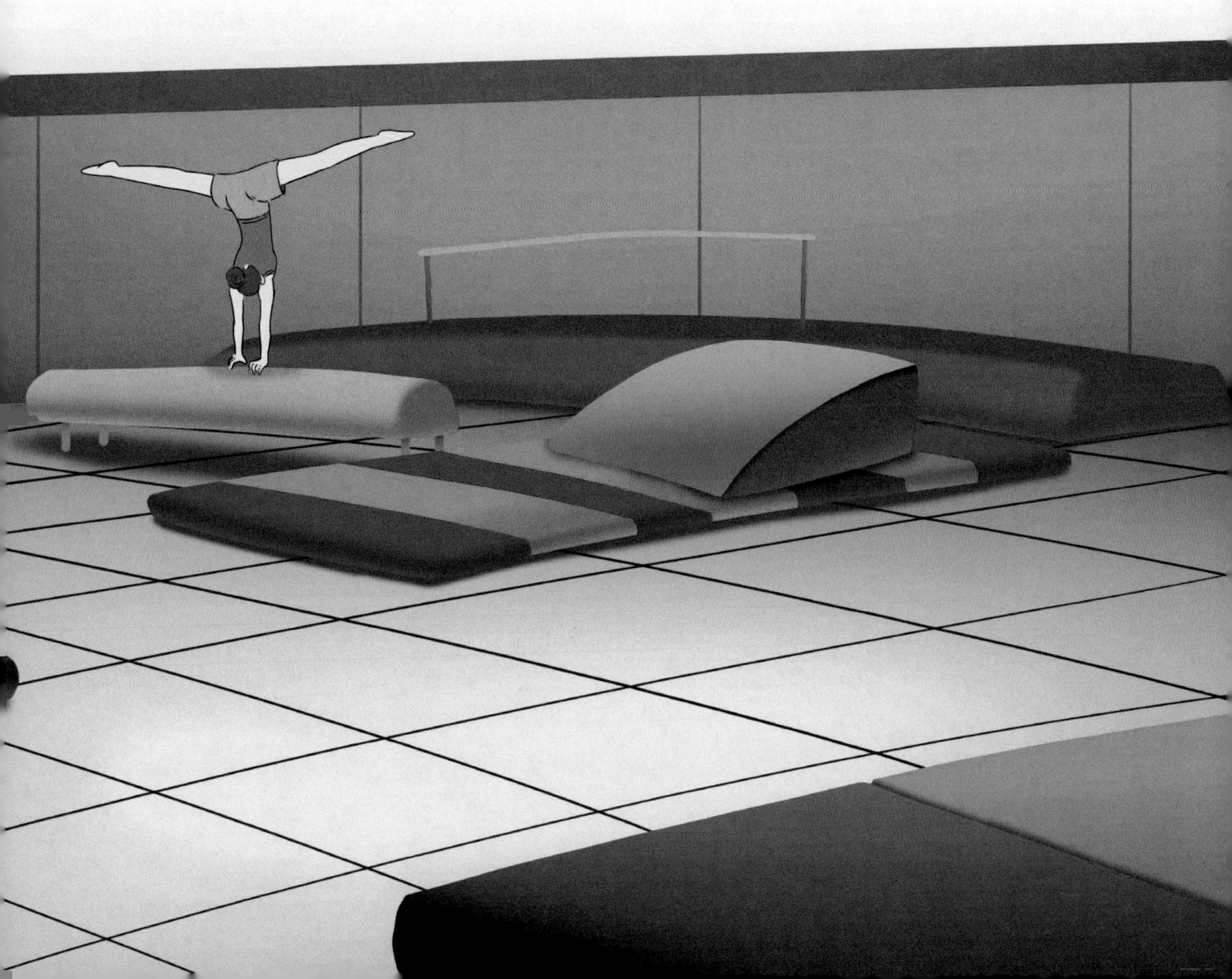

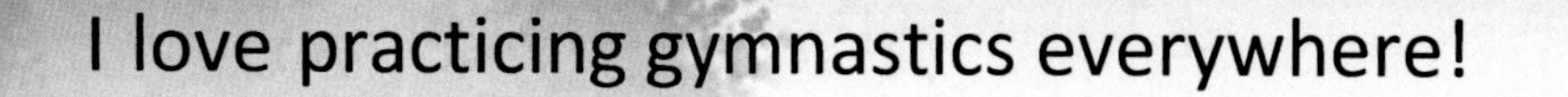

I love practicing gymnastics everywhere!

My favorite moves are doing Aerials and Handstands.

I can't think of a place that I haven't practiced: I practice at home in my bedroom, living room, basement, front and back yard.

I even practice at school during recess.

At G-Mommy's house and

I also practice at Jazzy G and Grandpa's house when I visit them in Akron, Ohio.

I can't wait to visit Auntie Marion in New York. There is a park across the street from her house. That would be the greatest place to practice doing back handsprings.

Normally, when my family goes to the park, we have to find one with a basketball hoop because my brother loves basketball.

I usually shoot hoops with him for a little bit, then I look for an open space to practice my front flips and back tucks.

Although I practice a lot, I still make mistakes.

Just the other day, I was working on perfecting my front flip but I kept stumbling when I landed.

I kept trying and trying, but I just couldn't get it right.

As I was getting frustrated, I could hear my Dad's voice say, "Son, slow down, but don't give up. Making mistakes is natural. It's how we learn."

After a couple more tries, I did it! A perfect landing!

The more I attended classes and practiced, the more confident and better I became.

After a while, I was able to move up to the intermediate boys' class. Some of the coaches noticed my natural talent and began holding me back after class to help fine tune some of my skills.

With more instruction and practice, I finally made it to the advanced boys' class.

One day after class, one of the coaches approached my parents and told them that I was really good and talented.

They were amazed at my improvement from the time I first began classes.

Then my coach asked my parents if I could be on the boys' gymnastics team.

I was so excited, but my parents were unsure.

My parents said that being on the team was a serious commitment.

Then they jokingly said, "If you are on the team, that means the whole family will be on the team."

They smiled at me and said, "Let's take a little more time to think about it."

I smiled even though I was disappointed and said, "Okay!"

Unfortunately, my parents did not sign me up for the team but they did take me to a boys' gymnastics competition so I could get an idea of what it would be like to be on the team.

It was so cool to see the boys that I practice with every Saturday competing, but I wish I could be competing with them, too.

My Mom and Dad said that one day soon, I will be able to be on the team.

I just wonder when that day will be.

I hope it will be soon. I just can't wait to be apart of the team.

The following Saturday, we went to watch another competition. I kept thinking, "When will it be my turn?"

Then came the biggest surprise. My coach came out to the seats and said, "Hey JD, what are you doing sitting there."

"We need you on the team."

"Your Mom and Dad think you're ready, so you better get geared up."

Wow! It was finally my turn to be a part of the team and help them to succeed in a competition.

We all did so well, and I won first place for my floor routine! I couldn't believe it!

I was so proud of myself, and my family was amazed at all of the things that I could do.

It feels great to finally be a part of the team.

I remember when at first all I wanted to do was flip and now I get to flip every day!

Dear Parents,

I would like to personally thank you for purchasing and taking the time to read my book. It is my belief that one of our responsibilities as parents is to facilitate opportunities that allow our children to identify, explore and develop their natural talents. We all have heard the saying, "there is no handbook when it comes to raising children." The journey is expected to be challenging and frustrating at times, however there are beautiful moments and memories that will be created along the way that make the journey worthwhile. When I was a kid, I grew up playing and loving "traditional" sports like basketball, football, and baseball, so it was shocking when my 7 year old son told me that he wanted to do gymnastics. My wife and I had no previous knowledge about this sport. Our only reference was watching women's gymnastics on TV every four years during the summer Olympics. So, we decided to educate ourselves and seek out a place that would allow our son to explore and cultivate his natural talent for flipping. I am glad that I did not allow my lack of knowledge and personal bias stop me from supporting my son and giving him the opportunity to participate in the sport that he loves. I hope that this book will give parents and children the courage to think and try things that are considered to be outside of the box.

Best Wishes,

I JUST WANT TO FLIP.

Made in the USA
Middletown, DE
11 January 2022